TOO PURPLEY!

To Sarah,
whose jammies were
always too scratchy
—J. R.

For Lucy,
in the sky
—G. L.

ISBN 978-0-545-49758-9

Text copyright © 2010 by Jean Reidy.
Illustrations copyright © 2010 by Geneviève Leloup.
All rights reserved. Published by Scholastic Inc.,
557 Broadway, New York, NY 10012,
by arrangement with Bloomsbury USA Children's Books.
SCHOLASTIC and associated logos are trademarks
and/or registered trademarks of Scholastic Inc.

12 11 10 9 8 7 6 5 4 3 2 1   12 13 14 15 16 17/0

Printed in the U.S.A.   08

This edition first printing, September 2012

Art created in Adobe Illustrator
Typeset in Keener
Book design by Geneviève Leloup

TOO PURPLEY!

JEAN REIDY

ILLUSTRATED BY GENEVIÈVE LELOUP

NOOOOOOOOOOO

SCHOLASTIC INC.

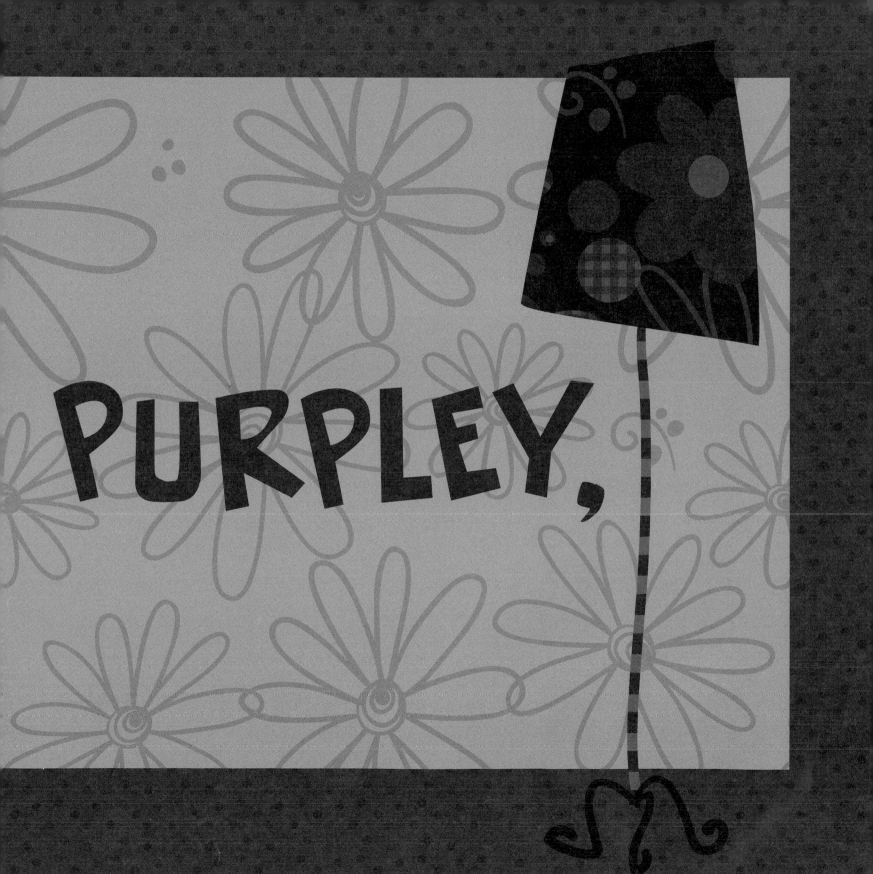

PURPLEY,

TOO PRICKLY.

TOO ITCHY,

TOO SCRATCHY,

TOO STITCHY,

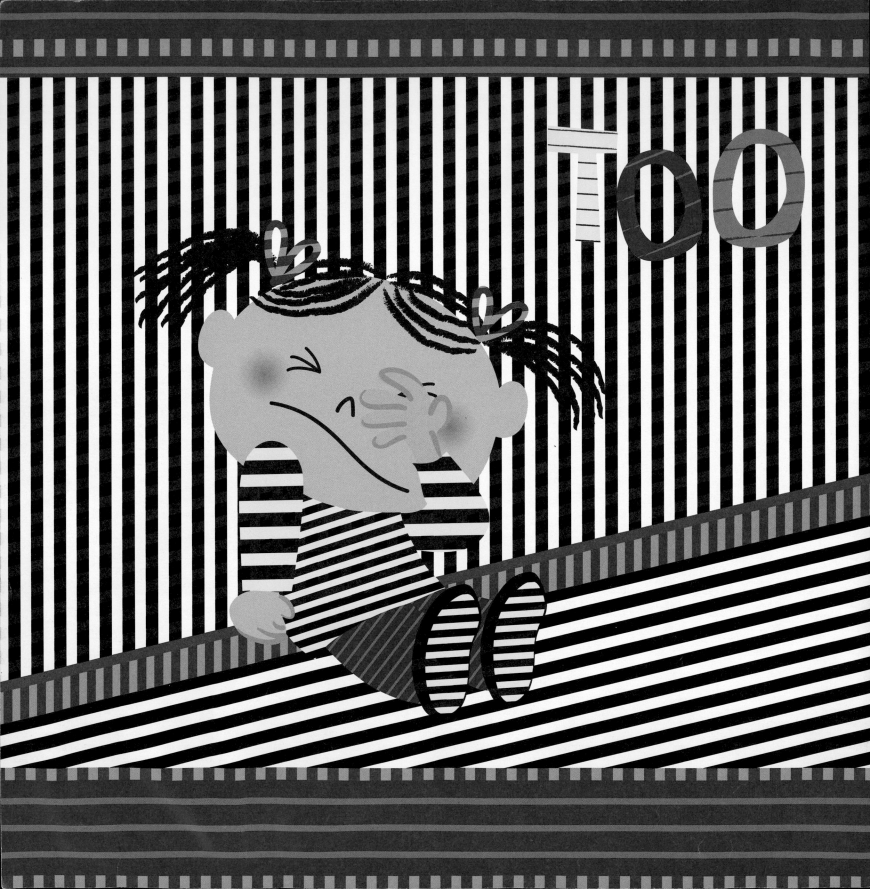

TOO TAGGY,

TOO STRAPPY,

TOO FEATHERY,

TOO
DANCEY,

TOO
LEATHERY,

TOO
FANCY.

TOO...

Jean Reidy hates too-snuggy jeans and prefers sweatpants. She writes from her home in Greenwood Village, Colorado, where she lives with her husband, Mike. Her four children and hordes of nieces and nephews provide her endless inspiration. *Too Purpley!* is her first picture book. Please visit her at www.jeanreidy.com.

Geneviève Leloup studied graphic arts, animation, and printing in Belgium, where she was born. Her whimsical illustrations have appeared in magazines and on various products, including lots of textiles and children's clothing. When not drawing or traveling, she bakes large amounts of cookies and plays accordion in her Brooklyn digs. She loved working on her first book.